First Experiences

THE NEW BABY

Anne Civardi
Illustrated by Stephen Cartwright

Consultant: Betty Root

There is a little yellow duck hiding on every two pages. Can you find it?

The Bunns

This is the Bunn family. Lucy is five and Tom is three.
Their Mum is going to have a baby soon.

he Bunn's House

GRANNY
AND
GRANDPA
BUNN

his is their house. Granny and Grandpa have come to
ook after Lucy and Tom while Mum is in hospital.

The Baby's Bedroom

There is a lot to do before the baby is born. Mum and Dad are busy getting the baby's bedroom ready.

Lucy and Tom are helping too. Mum is painting their old
cot for the baby to sleep in.

The Baby is Coming

Mum wakes up in the middle of the night. She feels the baby will be born soon.

Dad gets ready to take her to hospital while Grandpa rings to say Mum is on her way.

The Baby is Born

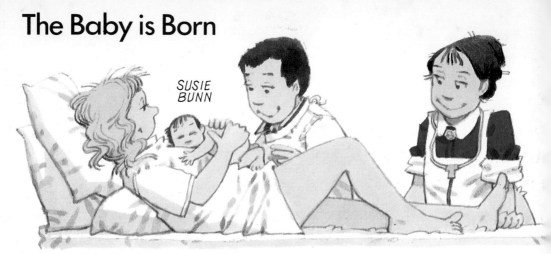

The baby has just been born. It is a girl. Mum and Dad are very happy. They will call her Susie.

Nurse Cherry weighs Susie to see how heavy she is and measures her to see how long she is.

usie is wrapped in a shawl to keep her warm. She has
name tag on her tiny wrist.

As soon as Dad gets home, he tells Lucy and Tom all
about baby Susie. They are longing to see her.

Visiting the Baby

The next day, Dad takes Lucy and Tom to the hospital to see their Mum and baby sister.

Mum is in a room with other Mums. They all have new babies. Which Mum has twins?

Coming Home

After a few days, Dad brings Mum and Susie home.
Everyone is excited and wants to hold the baby.

Susie is very sleepy. Mum is tired too. She will need a lot of help from Lucy, Tom and Dad.

Feeding Susie

When Susie is hungry, Mum feeds her with milk. Susie will need lots of feeds each day.

athing Susie

Now it is time for Susie's bath. Lucy loves to help Dad wash and dry her.

Going Out

Mum and Dad, Lucy and Tom take Susie for a walk.
They are all very pleased with the new baby.

First published in 1985
Usborne Publishing Ltd
20 Garrick St, London
WC2 9BJ, England
© Usborne Publishing Ltd 1985

The name of Usborne and the
device 🐝 are Trade Marks of
Usborne Publishing Ltd.

Printed in Portugal